For Jonah and Grandma ~ J.C.

tiger tales

5 River Road, Suite 128, Wilton, CT 06897

Published in the United States 2017

Originally published in Great Britain 2017 as *Love Enough for Two*

by Little Tiger Press

Text and illustrations copyright © 2017 Jane Chapman

Visit Jane Chapman at www.ChapmanandWarnes.com

ISBN-13: 978-1-68010-042-6

ISBN-10: 1-68010-042-4

Printed in China

LTP/1400/1646/0816

For more insight and activities, visit us at www.tigertalesbooks.com

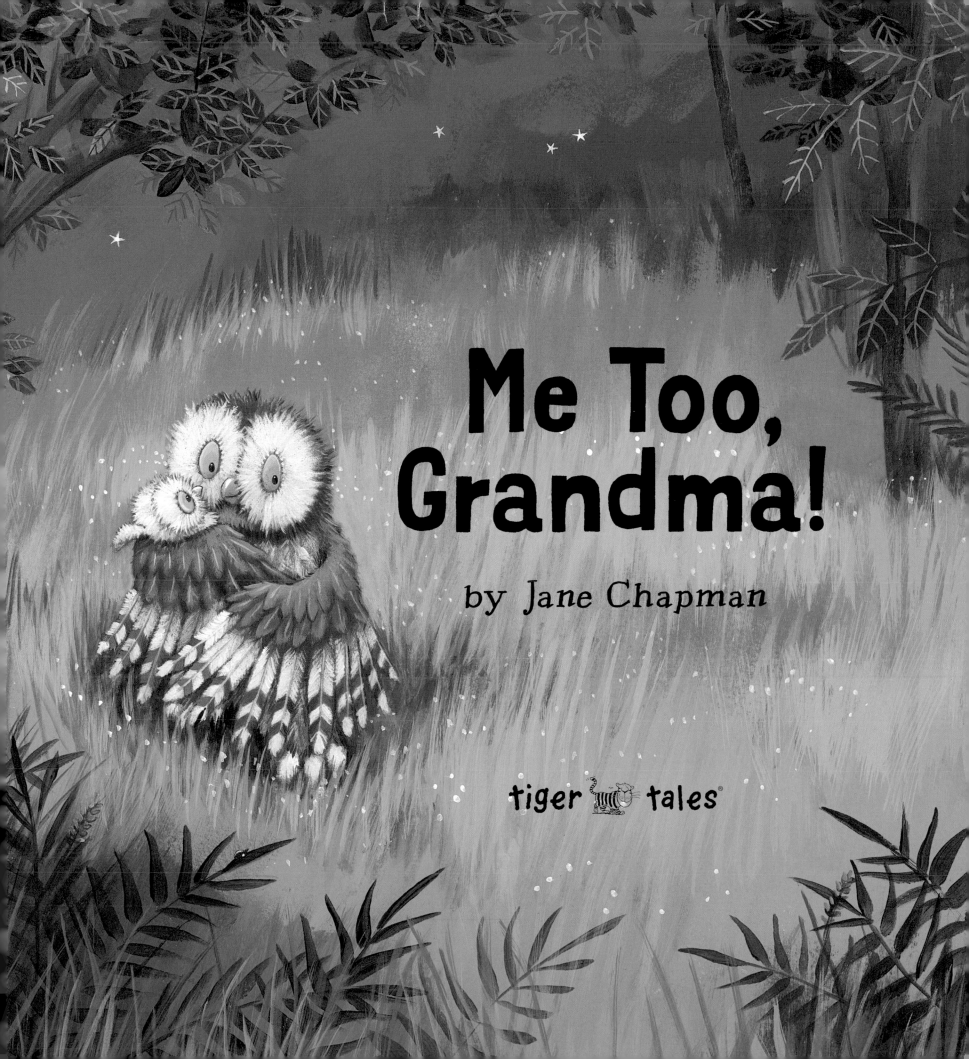

Me Too, Grandma!

by Jane Chapman

tiger tales

"Ollie!" called Grandma one evening. "I have a wonderful surprise for you!"

"Hoo-hoo! A surprise!" said Ollie. "I wonder what it could be . . . ."
He fluttered down excitedly to find out.

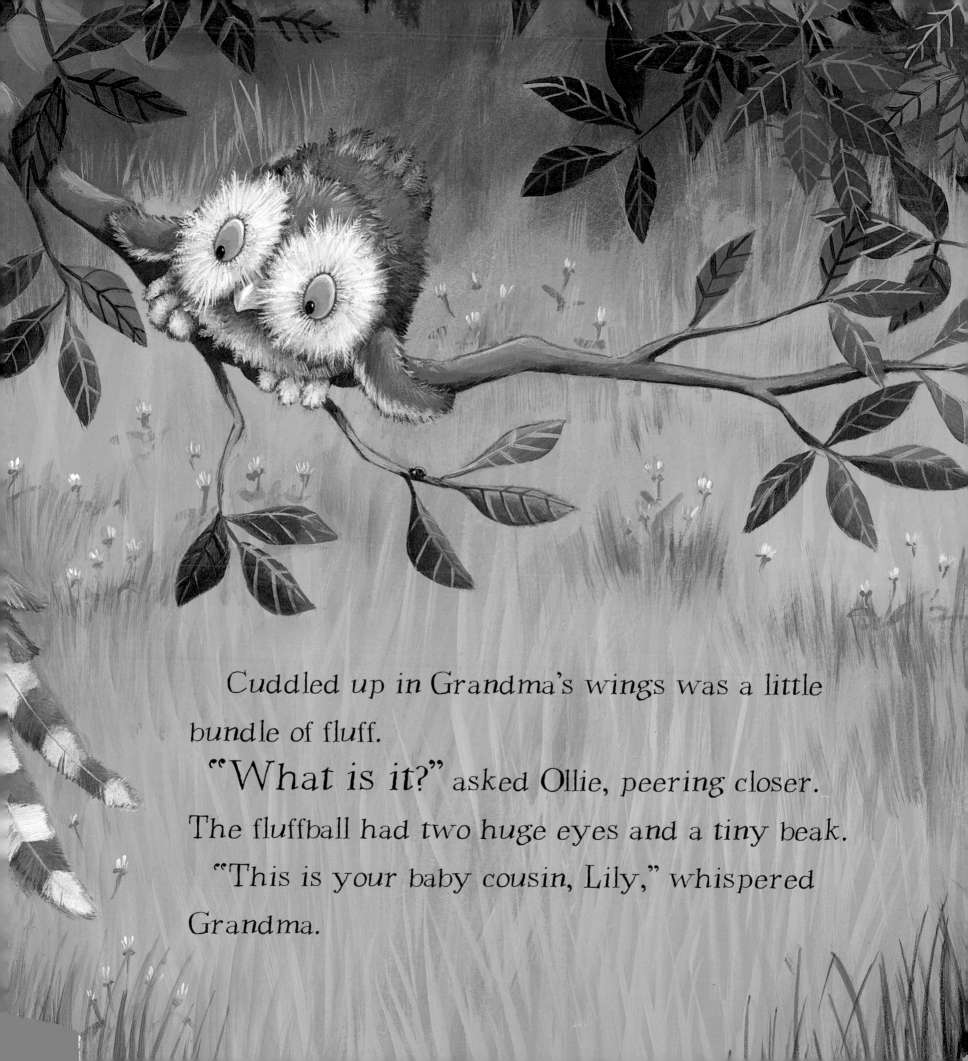

Cuddled up in Grandma's wings was a little bundle of fluff.

"What is it?" asked Ollie, peering closer. The fluffball had two huge eyes and a tiny beak.

"This is your baby cousin, Lily," whispered Grandma.

Lily stared at Ollie
and then blinked.

"She's not very chatty," muttered Ollie.
Grandma laughed. "Just say 'hi' and
maybe she'll wave—it's her new trick."
"Hi!" smiled Ollie.
"Hiya!" cheeped Lily, wiggling fluffy
feathers at him.

Grandma clapped proudly.
"Who's my little honeybun?" she cooed.
Honeybun? thought Ollie.
But I'M Grandma's
little honeybun!

"Can Lily play games?" asked Ollie.
"Well, she's very little . . .," chuckled Grandma,
"but I know she'd love to play with a big-boy owl like you."
"How about bunnyhops?" Ollie cheeped.
"You play it like this, Lily. . . hop! Hop! Hop!"

Ollie bounced around like
a ping-pong ball, but Lily
was a terrible hopper.

She just flopped
over backward.

"Owww!"
she squeaked.

"My poor sweetie!" soothed Grandma, scooping Lily up and tickling her tufty tummy until she chirped with delight.

"Hmmph!" Ollie grumped. His wings sagged a little bit. "Poor sweetie? What about me?"

"Let's push Lily in the swing," smiled Grandma. "You used to love it when you were little."

"Me first!" yelled Ollie, racing on ahead.

But Ollie was too big.
"Big boys need big swings!"
said Grandma. "This one is
for baby owls like Lily.
Ready, sweetness?"

Ollie watched Grandma push Lily back and forth.
"Look, Ollie—Lily thinks she's flying!" Grandma
hooted. "Would you like to push her?"

But Ollie was thinking. "Lily likes playing in the swing, doesn't she? So we can play hide-and-seek while she's busy! Start counting, Grandma!" And he fluttered off.

"Wait, Ollie!" called Grandma. "Lily's too little to swing on her own." "But I want to play with YOU, not Lily!" squawked Ollie. "Can't we put her down for a nap?"

"Let's have a snack instead," said Grandma. "That's something we can all do together."

Ollie flopped down on the
grass and waited for Grandma
to come back.

"Hiya! Hiya!" waved Lily,
but Ollie didn't feel like
waving back.

"Snack time!" smiled Grandma, breaking a cookie in half. "Here's a treat for my two little treasures."

Ollie looked down at his half
of the cookie. Suddenly, a tear
trickled down his beak, and
he covered his face to
hide his sniffles.

"You used to give me a whole
cookie, Grandma!" he cried.
"Don't you love me with your
whole heart anymore?"

"Oh, my little munchkin!" said Grandma.
"Is that what you've been thinking?"

Grandma sat Ollie on her lap for
a sniffly snuggle.

"I gave you only half a cookie
because it was the last one in the
box," she explained.

"But now you've got Lily...
and I'm not little like Lily
anymore," whimpered Ollie.

"Well, that's true!" laughed Grandma.
"You certainly are a big boy, but no matter
how big you get, you'll always be my
perfect little snuggle bug."

Ollie sniffed again and cuddled in closer.

"Let me tell you something amazing," Grandma continued. "When a new baby comes along, a grandma grows new love! Lily hasn't taken away any of my love for you."

"I didn't know that about grandmas," Ollie sniffled.

"Feel better?" asked Grandma.

But Ollie was looking at

his baby cousin.

"Hiya! Hiya!" cheeped Lily.

She was covered in crumbs from head to toe.

"Oh, my! This owlet needs a bath!" laughed Grandma.

"But watch out, Ollie—Lily loves to splash . . . ."

"Just like ME!" cheered Ollie.
"Come on, Lily—let's splash Grandma!"

Splish!

Splash!

Splosh!